DELETE

WATERCRESS

In memory of my parents,
Agnes Shiao-Fung Lee and Edward Chungman Chan,
immigrants and inspirations.
我永遠感謝你們。 —*A.W.*

For my father —*J.C.*

Neal Porter Books

Text copyright © 2021 by Andrea Wang

Illustrations copyright © 2021 by Jason Chin

All Rights Reserved

HOLIDAY HOUSE is registered in the U.S. Patent and Trademark Office.

Printed and bound in February 2022 at Toppan Leefung, DongGuan City, China.

The artwork for this book was made using watercolor on

140 pound cold press Saunders watercolor paper.

Book design by Jennifer Browne

www.holidayhouse.com

First Edition

10 9 8 7 6

Library of Congress Cataloging-in-Publication Data

Names: Wang, Andrea, author. | Chin, Jason, 1978– illustrator.

Title: Watercress / by Andrea Wang ; illustrated by Jason Chin.

Description: First edition. | New York : Holiday House, [2021] | "A Neal
    Porter Book." | Audience: Ages 4 to 8. | Audience: Grades K–1. |

Summary: Embarrassed about gathering watercress from a roadside ditch,
a girl learns to appreciate her Chinese heritage after learning why
the plant is so important to her parents.

Identifiers: LCCN 2020017366 | ISBN 9780823446247 (hardcover)

Subjects: CYAC: Watercress—Fiction. | Harvesting—Fiction. | Chinese
Americans—Fiction. | Family life—Ohio—Fiction. | Ohio—Fiction.

Classification: LCC PZ7.1.W3645 Wat 2021 | DDC [E]—dc23

LC record available at https://lccn.loc.gov/2020017366

ISBN 978-0-8234-4624-7 (hardcover)

WATERCRESS

ANDREA WANG

PICTURES BY JASON CHIN

NEAL PORTER BOOKS

HOLIDAY HOUSE / NEW YORK

FX 9-23

We are in the old Pontiac,
the red paint faded by years of
glinting Ohio sun,
pelting rain,
and biting snow.

The tops of the cornstalks make
lines that zigzag
across the horizon.
Mom shouts,
"Look!"
and the car comes to
an abrupt, jerking stop.

Mom's eyes are as sharp as
the tip of
a dragon's claw.

Dad's eyes grow wide.
"Watercress!" they exclaim,
two voices
heavy with memories.

From the depths of the trunk,
they unearth
a brown paper bag,
rusty scissors,

and a longing for
China.

They haul us out of the back seat.
We are told to
untie our sneakers,
peel off our socks,
and roll up our jeans.

We have to help them gather it.

The water in the ditch is cold.
It stings my ankles
and the mud squelches
up between my toes.

A car passes by
and I duck my head
hoping it's
no one I know.

My parents cut bunches of the small plant,
long stringy stems with
leaves round as coins.

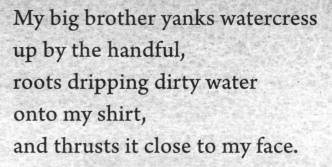

My big brother yanks watercress
up by the handful,
roots dripping dirty water
onto my shirt,
and thrusts it close to my face.

There are tiny snails
clinging to the
underside.

I squirm away.

The bag in my hands grows
heavier
and heavier
with the weight of all
the watercress.

The paper is soaked and I'm
half afraid
half hopeful
that the bottom will split,
sending all the plants back down
into the muck.

Finally, we load everything,
the soggy bag,
my sopping shirt,
our sodden selves,
into the car and head home.
Our original destination is long
forgotten,
a memory of something
unfinished.

On the dinner table that night is a dish
of watercress,
glistening with garlicky oil and
freckled with sesame seeds.

The mud and the snails are
long gone
but I still don't want to eat it.
Any of it.

I only want to eat vegetables from
the grocery store.

Mom and Dad press me to try some.
"It is fresh," Dad says.
"It is free," Mom says.
I shake my head.

Free is bad.
Free is
hand-me-down clothes and

roadside trash-heap furniture and
now,
dinner from a ditch.

Mom sighs and disappears
into her room,
returning with an old photo.

"My family," she says,
"from before."
We stare.
Mom never talks about her China family.

She points to a small boy
as thin as a stem of watercress.
"My little brother. Your uncle."
We hold our breaths.
Mom never told us what happened to him.

"During the great
famine," she says,
"we ate anything
we could find,

but it was still
not enough."

I look from my uncle's hollow face
to the watercress on the table
and I am ashamed of
being ashamed of
my family.

I take a bite of the watercress and
it bites me back with
its spicy, peppery taste.
It is delicate and
slightly bitter,

like Mom's memories
of home.

Together,
we eat it
all
and make a
new memory of
watercress.

A NOTE FROM THE AUTHOR

This story is about the power of memory. Not just the beautiful memories, like the ones my mother and father had about eating watercress in China, but also the difficult ones, the memories that are sometimes too painful to share. It starts with my own distressing memory of being made to pick watercress that was growing wild by the side of the road. As the child of Chinese immigrants, growing up in a small, mostly white town in Ohio, I was very aware of how different my family and I were from everyone else. It's hard to feel like you don't belong, and collecting food from a muddy roadside ditch just made that bad feeling more intense for me—something my very practical parents didn't understand.

When I was young, my parents didn't talk about their memories of China, of growing up poor, losing siblings, and surviving war. I don't blame them—these are difficult topics to discuss with children. But it's important, too, for children to understand their family history. Perhaps if I had known about the hardships they had faced, I would have been more compassionate as a child. Maybe I would have felt more empathy and less anger. More pride in my heritage and less shame. Memories have the power to inform, to inspire, and to heal.

This story is both an apology and a love letter to my parents. It's also an encouragement to all children who feel different and to families with difficult pasts—share your memories. Tell your stories. They are essential. —A. W.

A NOTE FROM THE ARTIST

When I first read *Watercress*, I was impressed by how Andrea was able to fold so many layers of memory, culture, and emotion into a short text, and I wanted the illustrations to complement each of those layers. I wanted the art to reflect the American and Chinese heritage of the characters. I chose to paint in watercolor because it's common to both Chinese and western art and I used both Chinese and western brushes. The color palette is heavy in yellow ochre, which reminds me of old photographs and 1970s decor, and cerulean blue, which is similar to the blue often used in Chinese paintings. Traditional Chinese landscape paintings feature mountains painted with soft marks that create a dreamlike quality. This technique seemed appropriate for implying memory, so I included many soft washes throughout the book.

It is common for children of immigrants to be unaware of their parents' stories and culture, and to feel out of place, misunderstood, and even angry. My own father, also a child of Chinese immigrants, rejected Chinese food when he was young in an effort to try and fit in. These feelings, especially the anxiety that comes from feeling different, are not limited to immigrants and their children—they are universal. When I was painting, I drew on my own memories of exclusion, loss, and guilt with the hope that they might seep into the art and add another layer to Andrea's remarkable story. —J. C.